FOR MY MUM AND DAD - K.G.

OXFORD
UNIVERSITY PRESS

Great Clarendon Street, Oxford OX2 6DP

Oxford University Press is a department of the University of Oxford.
It furthers the University's objective of excellence in research,
scholarship, and education by publishing worldwide in

Oxford   New York

Auckland Cape Town Dar es Salaam Hong Kong Karachi
Kuala Lumpur Madrid Melbourne Mexico City Nairobi
New Delhi Shanghai Taipei Toronto

With offices in

Argentina Austria Brazil Chile Czech Republic France Greece
Guatemala Hungary Italy Japan Poland Portugal Singapore
South Korea Switzerland Thailand Turkey Ukraine Vietnam

Oxford is a registered trade mark of Oxford University Press
in the UK and in certain other countries

Text and illustrations © Karen George 2013

The moral rights of the author/illustrator have been asserted
Database right Oxford University Press (maker)

First published in 2013

British Library Cataloguing in Publication Data
Data available

ISBN: 978-0-19-913737-4 (hardback)
ISBN: 978-0-19-913738-1 (paperback)

10 9 8 7 6 5 4 3 2 1

Printed in China

Paper used in the production of this book is a natural,
recyclable product made from wood grown in sustainable forests.
The manufacturing process conforms to the environmental
regulations of the country of origin.

Display typography on cover, page 1, page 4, and page 5 uses
Lady Rene © Sudtipos

HOR
CM

HUGH SHAMPOO

Karen George

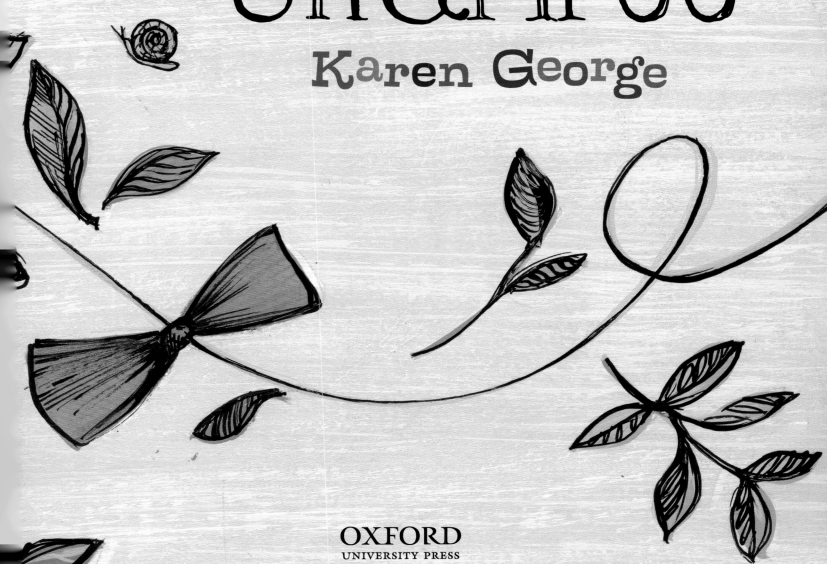

OXFORD
UNIVERSITY PRESS

If you think having your hair
washed is horrid, then
you should meet . . .
Hugh Shampoo!

His hair was terribly tangled
and very, **very** grubby but Hugh didn't care!

He would not
have his hair
washed
or brushed
or cut
or combed
or in
any way
fussed with.

Whenever Hugh's mum and dad tried to wash...

brush, cut, or comb....

his hair, they failed!

This upset
Mr and Mrs Shampoo.

After all, they were both . . .

Teacups tinkled, hairdryers hummed,
and friends chatted, while
Mr and Mrs Shampoo's scissors
went snippety snip all day long.

One teatime, Mrs Shampoo showed Hugh an extremely exciting letter. 'Dear Team Shampoo,' she read. 'You are in the final of the **SCISSOR SHOWDOWN**!' 'We made it!' cheered Mr Shampoo. 'Now we just need someone to model our wonderful winning styles.'

slurp!

Hugh longed to be part of Team Shampoo,
but not if it meant having **his** hair washed!

So whose hair could the Shampoos use?

they could . . .

tease and twirl . . .

Mrs Tree's hair.

The Shampoos could not lose!

The next day, Mr and Mrs Shampoo collected bottles
and brushes, combs and curlers, teacups and towels,
and everything they needed for the **SCISSOR SHOWDOWN**.

'Mrs Tree, we'll meet you in the town hall at three,' they said.

And off they went, leaving grubby-haired Hugh to help Mr Tree trim the hedge.

But, later, just as Mrs Tree was about to leave for the **SCISSOR SHOWDOWN**, there was a scream!

'Mr Tree!' she shrieked. 'My hair . . . it's gone! All chopped off! What a disaster!

Run Hugh!
Tell Team Shampoo . . .

all is lost!'

So Hugh ran.
He blasted past
rose bushes . . .

He parted long grass
like a comb through
clean hair.

His legs flew as fast as
snippety snipping scissors.

He ran full tilt, as if blown
by a hundred hairdryers.

But when Hugh reached
the town hall, he thought
he was too late.

SCISSOR

SHOWDOWN

The judge began to speak. 'And the winner of the **SCISSOR SHOWDOWN** is . . .

Team Shampoo

for their spectacular show-stopping styling
of Hugh Shampoo!'

That night Hugh went to bed with the winner's cup.

But he also went to bed with

the roses,

the grass,

the butterflies,

the kite strings,

the itchy leaves,

the sticky bubble gum,

the wriggling worms,

and the slimy snails!

'Aaargh!
Yuck!'

cried Hugh.

'I need . . .

shampoo!'

For his mum and dad it was a dream come true. They washed,

they brushed,

they combed,

they snipped .

and they hugged their very own

Hugh Shampoo!